W9-AFA-031

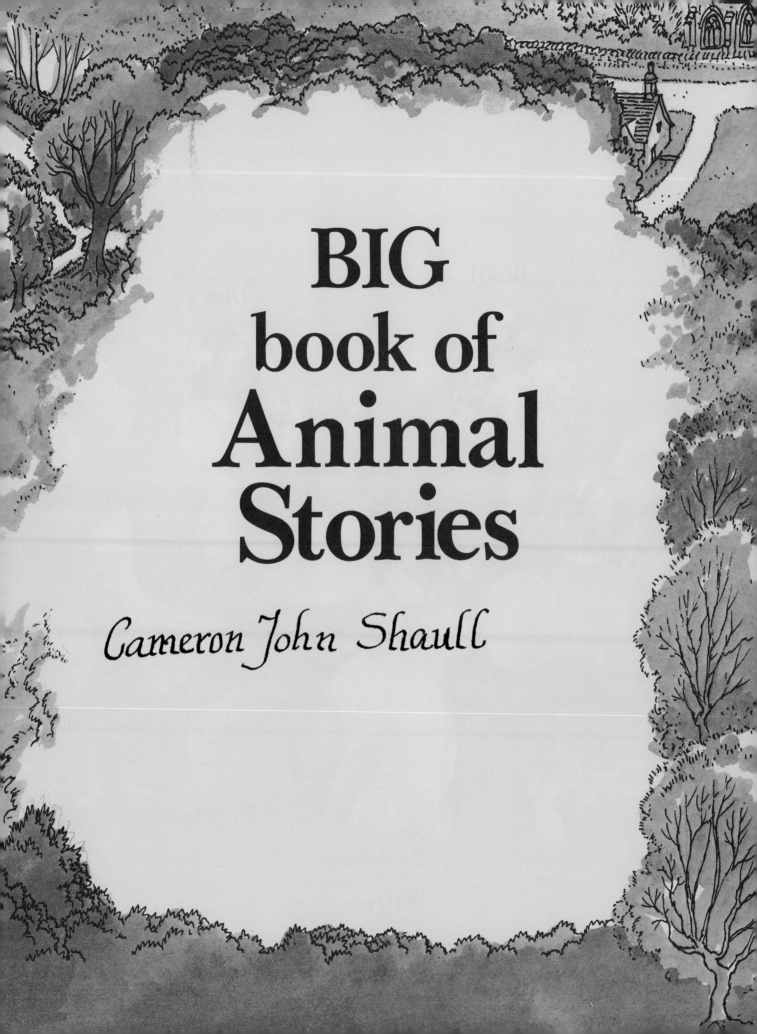

BIG
book of
Animal
Stories

Cameron John Shaull

Basil

Dewy

Willie

BIG
book of
Animal
Stories

Lucy Kincaid

Illustrated by Eric Kincaid

BRIMAX · NEWMARKET · ENGLAND

ISBN 0 86112 359 X
© BRIMAX BOOKS LTD 1986. All rights reserved
Published by BRIMAX BOOKS, Newmarket, England
This book is an enlarged edition of 'Animal Bedtime Stories'
Fourth printing 1990
Printed in Portugal By Edições ASA—Divisão Gráfica

CONTENTS

MOVING IN

Ash Lodge had been empty for years. Smoke never
curled from its chimney. The shutters never opened to
let in the sunlight. The grey slates had gathered moss
and dry brown leaves lay in thick piles against its walls.
It was a lonely, babes-in-the-wood, kind of house.

But all that was about to change.

One morning there was the sound of voices, and the rumble of wheels rolling over cracking twigs. Two badgers were pulling a handcart, loaded with belongings, along the overgrown path which led towards the house.

"How much further is it?" enquired a voice from somewhere behind the pile of tables and chairs and beds. Willie Mole was sitting on the back of the cart, swinging his short little legs. His badger friends were big strong fellows, no point in a little mole like him thinking he could help.

"We're there," said Dewy and Basil in one breath.

Willie slithered to the ground in an untidy heap as the end of the cart came to rest on the ground.

"You might have warned me," he grumbled as he picked himself up.

Basil and Dewy were walking around the little house, shuffling their feet through the thick carpet of leaves and peeping through cracks in the shutters. Willie shuffled after them like a miniature steam engine, spraying leaves to the left and to the right. They made a full circle round the house and arrived back at the front door.

"Let's go inside," said Willie.

"Give me the key then," said Basil.

Willie looked at him blankly.

"We gave it to you to look after, remember?"

Willie shook his head. Not because he didn't remember, because he did, but because he'd forgotten what he had done with the key. "I ... er ... ummm ..."

Basil and Dewy exchanged glances and sighed.

"It's our own fault ... we should have known better," said Basil. "Let's see if there is another way in ... and meanwhile ..." Basil glared at Willie, "... you just try to remember what you did with it."

Willie sat on the porch and gave a very good impression of someone thinking. His brow was creased and his eyes half closed, but what he was really thinking was, "I hope they hurry up and get us in," and not about the lost key at all. His friends completed another full circle of the house.

"No way in . . ." they informed Willie. "Unless you . . . ?"

Willie shook his head.

"Then there is only one thing to do," said Basil.

"Oh dear!" wailed Willie. "We're not going to push the cart all the way back, are we?"

"Shsh . . ." said Dewy. "Basil's thinking."

Basil seemed to be measuring distances with his eye. Distances between the tree and the roof. Presently he took a coil of rope from the cart and with an expert throw looped one end over an overhanging branch.

The next moment Willie found himself with the rope tied round his middle, dangling in mid air, and going up, rapidly.

"What am I doing up here?" he cried in alarm.

"You're going down the chimney," said Basil.

"No I'm not," said Willie.

Obviously Dewy and Basil thought otherwise.

13

"We'll lower you very carefully . . . we promise . . ." they
said. And they did. Very carefully. And Willie disappeared down the chimney. When the rope went slack they
let go of their end and rapped at the front door.

"Wod ab I subbosed do do now I'b in here?" asked a
complaining voice from behind the door.

"Open the door, and let us in, you fool . . ." said Basil.
Slowly the door swung open. Willie was covered from
head to foot in soot. His once shiny fur was dull, his
tiny eyes watering, his nose twitching violently.

"Atishoo! Atishoo! AtishOOOOO!" A cloud of black dust danced all round him, then enfolded him again like a well fitting glove. "I hobe you're sadisfied . . ." he said, as though he had a bad cold in his nose.

"We'll soon clean you up," said Basil. He untied the rope, and while Dewy swept up the pile of soot in the fire-place, he gave Willie a quick sweep over with the yard broom, which happened to be the first thing he found.

"Ouch!" said Willie. "Atishoooo!" said Willie.

"Stop complaining . . ." said Basil.

By suppertime everything had been unpacked and there was a tasty stew simmering in a pot over the open fire.

Willie found the lost key in his sponge bag with his toothbrush and when he found it, of course, he remembered putting it there. He put it on the mantelpiece and pretended he didn't know how it had got there but he didn't fool Dewy or Basil one little bit.

"Two of us came through the door anyway," laughed Basil.

Willie was going to say something rude but his nose was still tickling and a sudden fit of sneezing made him forget what he was going to say, which maybe was just as well.

WILLIE AND THE BEES

A few days after the badgers and Willie moved in, Ash Lodge had a visitor. She flew into the kitchen and buzzed around as though she was thinking of moving in too.

"Go away . . . go away . . ." shouted Willie, waving his paws wildly around his head as though he was sending messages in semaphore. "Keep away from me you bully . . . keep away."

Basil appeared in the doorway.

"Who are you talking to?" he asked.

"Make it go away . . ." shouted Willie.

"Make what go away?" asked Basil patiently.

"That . . . that thing," said Willie, pointing to the bee who was now walking round the top of a jampot. He hoped it wouldn't fall in. If it did he would never eat jam again.

"But it's only a bee," said Basil. "You're not really afraid of bees."

"Yes I am," said Willie. "Bees are nasty, unfriendly creatures, they buzz . . ."

Basil sighed and opened the kitchen window.

"Take my advice and fly away while you are still safe," he said to the bee and shooed her into the garden.

Dewy, who had been outside all morning, saw Basil at the window and called, "Come and see what I've found."

Dewy had found some more bees. A whole swarm of them, high in the branches of a tree.

"I'm going to get them down," he said.

He had already put a ladder against the tree and now
he climbed up towards the swarm. It buzzed alarmingly.
"You're not going to bring them down here, are you?"
screeched Willie. He didn't wait for a reply. He knew
the answer. He dived head first into a pile of leaves.

"What's the matter with him?" asked Dewy as he came down the ladder with the bees humming loudly inside his big straw hat.

"He's playing hide and seek," said Basil and dropped some more leaves onto Willie's back.

"Who with?" asked Dewy.

"The bees . . ." said Basil. "They dared to buzz."

"Oh I see," said Dewy with his own nose almost inside the straw hat with the bees. "These bees are looking for a new home." He understood about such things.

"Don't let them move in with US," called Willie from beneath his pile of leaves.

"Let's make them a hive," said Basil. "Then perhaps they will stay in the garden."

Willie resolved there and then to stay in the pile of leaves for ever. He was NEVER going to come out . . . not with a garden FULL of bees . . . nasty, buzzing creatures . . .

It didn't take Basil long to make a hive. He knew about such things, just as Dewy knew about things that had wings. When the hive was finished they set it up in a clearing close to the house.

"Please move in and make yourselves comfortable," said

Dewy, and he placed the straw hat beside the hive.

Willie couldn't believe his ears. "Talking to bees," he muttered, "why doesn't he talk to ME if he wants someone to talk to. I'm the one who is frightened." And he buried himself even deeper into his hide-away of leaves.

The bees moved into the hive immediately and within a few minutes were out again, collecting pollen and nectar.

"SHOULD HAVE SOME HONEY NEXT YEAR," said Dewy, rather loudly for someone who usually spoke rather quietly.

"HONEY!" said Willie. Willie liked honey. Did bees make honey? Perhaps they weren't such bad little things after all. Perhaps their buzz was not as bad as it sounded. He rose, with dignity, from his pile of leaves.

"They can stay if they want to," he said, "as long as they keep away from me and as long as they don't buzz too much."

"That's kind of you," said Basil and Dewy, who had known all the time that Willie would eventually get used to the bees. Things that buzzed always sent him into a panic for a while. They supposed it was because he was a mole. Perhaps he had sensitive ears.

21

A few days later Dewy called Basil and quietly led him into the wood. Willie was busy painting a portrait.
"You MUST sit still," he was saying to the bee who was posing for him. "And do try not to buzz QUITE so loudly." The two badgers smiled and crept quietly away.

THE RAFT

Dewy and Basil were sitting at breakfast one morning, their thoughts far away as they tried to decide what they were going to do with the day, when something Willie said decided it for them.

Willie said, "Let's make a boat."

Behind Ash Lodge there was a pond. A wide pond that curled between the trees and pretended to be a river. It was deep. They already knew that. Too deep to paddle in. When they had pushed in a pole to test the depth, the pole had come out covered in thick mud. No, definitely not a pond to paddle in. But a pond to sail on? Now that was a different matter altogether.

Willie danced around excitedly as Basil sorted out the wood he had in the shed.

"Not quite the right sort of thing for boat building," said Basil, "unless you'd like a patchwork boat."

Willie looked so disappointed Basil knew he would have to think of something. "There are plenty of logs lying about in the wood," he said. "We could make a raft."

Dewy and Basil spent the whole morning dragging logs through the wood and down to the edge of the pond. Willie was so excited he even helped a little bit himself.

When they had enough logs Basil sawed them all to the same length and then they tied the whole lot together with a rope in a series of loops and complicated knots. Willie, somehow, got caught in one loop and they had to untie three tightly tied knots that took a great deal of untying, to get him out.

"I sometimes think Willie is more helpful when he is not trying to help," sighed Basil as he tied them up again. "Now all we've got to do is find something to use as a paddle and then we can try it out."

While he was rummaging in the shed Dewy and Willie pushed the raft into the water.

"It floats . . . it floats . . ." cried Willie excitedly.

Now Dewy didn't think for a moment that Willie would be so silly, so what Willie did next was quite unexpected. He gave the raft a hefty push and then leapt onto it.

"I'm floating . . . I'm floating . . ." he cried.

Dewy tried to catch the raft before it drifted out into the pond and almost fell into the pond himself doing it. He couldn't reach.

"You silly, silly mole," he said.

The raft floated to the middle of the pond and there it stopped. It kept absolutely still. Nothing Willie did would make it move.

"Help . . . HELP . . ." he called.

"What are we going to do?" asked Dewy in despair.
"We need arms fifteen feet long to reach him out there."
They couldn't throw a rope. They had used the only rope
they had to tie the logs together.

"You'll have to swim," called Basil.

"I'm not leaving the raft," said Willie. "We might never get it back."

"We might never get YOU back if you don't," said Dewy.

Willie sat and sighed, and waited for Basil and Dewy to think of a way of rescuing him.

27

When rescue did come it came from an unexpected source. A family of ducks suddenly appeared round the bend in the pond. They were out for a swim and a gossip.

"Are you stranded?" they asked Willie politely, though it was perfectly obvious that he was. Willie nodded.

"Can you push the raft to the bank?" called Basil.

"In less time than it takes to quack," said the ducks.

They lined themselves up behind the raft, put their beaks down, paddled hard with their webbed feet, and pushed. The raft just skimmed across the water. As it bumped against the bank Basil and Dewy caught hold of it and pulled it onto firm ground.

"If you had waited until I found the paddle you would have been able to get yourself ashore," grumbled Basil.

"I'm sorry," said Willie, though he wasn't really. It was fun being pushed about on a raft by ducks.

Before he did anything else Basil found a piece of thick twine and tied the paddle firmly to the raft.

"Just to make sure it doesn't happen again . . . to any of us," he said. "The ducks might not be around to help next time."

AN UPSET TOAD

There was a huge stone jar lying on its side beside the pond. It was half buried in fallen leaves and Willie found it a good place to sit when he wanted to watch the fish swimming in the pond.

One morning when they were tidying the garden and sweeping up leaves Basil said,

"Let's see if we can push that jar upright. If we can perhaps we can plant something in it."

They cleared away all the leaves and then with Basil pushing, Dewy pulling, and Willie watching, they managed to get it onto its end.

"That was easier than I thought it was going to be," said Basil.

Willie walked round the jar in astonishment. He was surprised how tall it was. The top was as high as the tip of his nose. He stretched up on his tiptoes and was just about to take a look into its dark inside when it croaked.

Willie's eyes grew big and round.

"What was that?" he asked, and stepped back four paces very smartly indeed.

"It was me," croaked a voice from inside the jar.

"Who is me?" asked Basil as he stared down into the darkness. He saw two golden eyes looking back at him.

"There's someone in there," said Basil. "We'd better tip the jar over again so that whoever it is can get out."

He and Dewy carefully lowered the jar back onto its side.

Out jumped an 'ornery, and extremely cross, toad.

31

"How dare you tip my home up like that," he croaked.

"We didn't know you were in there," said Basil.

"Should have asked," croaked the toad.

"But how could we ask if we didn't know you were there," protested Dewy.

"That was your problem," croaked the toad. "Now go away and leave me alone. I've got lots of straightening to do. You've tipped everything into a terrible muddle."

"We're very sorry, I'm sure," said Dewy.

"Do you mean to say that every time I sat on that jar I was sitting on a toad?" gasped Willie. He looked at the toad's cross little face and wondered how he had ever dared to do such a risky thing. He felt quite weak at the knees and had to sit down quickly. The nearest thing, of course, was the jar, and without thinking he sat on that.

"Get off! Get off!" croaked the toad, jumping up and down on the spot like a yoyo without a string.

"It's our jar," protested Basil, standing between the frightened Willie and the angry toad.

"It's MY home!" croaked the toad.

"You're a squatter!" shouted Willie in a sudden burst

of courage, but he made quite sure Basil was standing between him and the toad.

"I'm not . . . I'm not . . ." croaked the toad, with just the suspicion of a sob in his voice.

"Let's sit down and talk this over," said Dewy calmly. "I'm sure we can come to some arrangement. I can quite understand how the toad feels," he said. "I'd feel the same if Ash Lodge was suddenly turned on its side with me inside it."

"Quite so . . ." said Basil thoughtfully. "I know I would and I'm sure Willie would too."

And Willie had to agree. He would not have liked it either. He held out his paw and smiled at the toad.

"Let's be friends," he said.

"Can I stay in my home?" asked the toad.

"Of course," said the badgers and Willie together.

"In that case," said the toad, turning to Willie, "you can sit on my roof and watch the fish whenever you like."

And that was how the badgers and Willie became friends with a neighbour they never knew they had until they upended the stone jar that lay beside the pond.

A NOISE IN THE NIGHT

It was a dark night. The moon was behind the clouds and most of the stars were hidden. It was still everywhere. And very quiet. Willie was in bed trying to get to sleep. At first he thought he had imagined the noise. Then he knew he hadn't and he sat up with his fur tingling.

He crept into Dewy's room and woke him.
"What's the matter?" asked Dewy sleepily. And then
he heard it too. Scrape . . . scrape . . . scrape . . . just above
their heads. Basil appeared in the doorway with his torch.
"This needs investigating," he said. "Follow me . . ."

"Perhaps it's burglars," whispered Willie, staying close enough to Dewy to be mistaken for his shadow.

"We'll soon find out," said Basil and picked up the poker from the fireplace . . . just in case.

"Why are we creeping around down here when the noise is coming from up there?" whispered Dewy.

"There might be an accomplice hiding behind an arm-chair," whispered Basil.

"ooo OOOH . . ." Willie clung even tighter to Dewy.

"Why don't we just put on the light?" asked Dewy.

". . . and frighten them away before we catch them!" said Basil, as though THAT was sufficient answer.

They searched the house from end to end . . . from corner to corner . . . they looked behind all the chairs and under all the mats. They even looked in the cupboard under the sink.

"Be careful," whispered Dewy as Willie trod on his heels. He was too late. As Willie stumbled his elbow caught the handle of a saucepan and it fell with a clatter to the floor.

"OOOWWW!" shouted Willie at the very top of his voice.

Willie's shout frightened the badgers more than the clatter of the saucepan.

"Shhhhh!" they said when their teeth had stopped chattering.

"Whoever it was prowling about is bound to have gone after hearing a noise like that," said Basil. "Come on, we might as well go back to bed and look for footprints and clues in the morning."

"Shhh!" said Willie suddenly, his fur standing absolutely on end. "Listen!"

They listened. Scrape . . . scrape . . . scrape . . . the noise was immediately above their heads. It was too much for Basil. He was tired of being scared. He raised the poker and banged its knob hard against the ceiling.

"Come down from there . . . whoever you are . . . do you hear me . . . come down . . ." he shouted.

Willie dived into the cupboard with the saucepans. The clatter he made was worse than an overhead thunderstorm.

"We are all going to stay together," said Dewy as he dragged him out again. "And stop making so much NOISE!"

"Be quiet BOTH of you, and listen," said Basil urgently.

"We'll meet you outside," called a squeaky voice from
above the ceiling. Poor Willie nearly died of fright, but
he was caught up between Basil and Dewy and rushed into the
garden. They were just in time to see five dark shapes fly
from a hole cut in the stonework under the eaves.

It was too much for Willie.

"G . . . g . . . ghosts . . ." he whispered, and fainted.

"Are they g.g.ghosts?" whispered Basil feeling rather faint himself. To his amazement Dewy walked straight up to the shapes who were now sitting huddled on a ledge.

Presently he came back with a broad smile on his face.

"It's alright," he said. "They didn't mean any harm. They thought the house was empty. They have been moving into the roof."

"They . . . THEY . . . who are THEY?" demanded Basil in a loud whisper.

"My friends the bats," said Dewy. "Come over and I'll introduce you."

Willie opened his eyes. "Please don't leave me," he whispered.

"There's nothing to be afraid of," said Dewy firmly. "The bats were just as frightened as you. It comes as a surprise when a house you think is empty starts making noises like an exploding saucepan factory. Now come and apologise to THEM."

Willie took a lot of persuading but at last everyone had apologised to everyone else and it was decided that the bats could stay in the roof as long as they promised to wear carpet slippers when they were moving about at night.

"We meet our neighbours in the strangest ways," sighed Willie as he went back to bed.

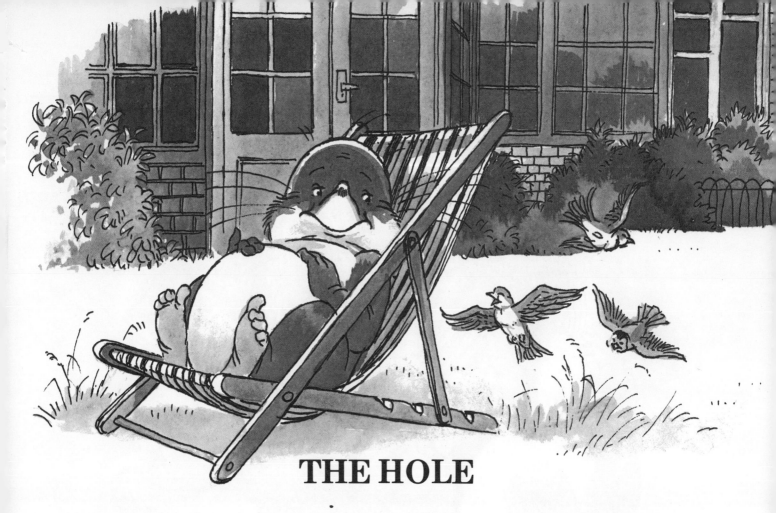

THE HOLE

It was sunny and hot. Willie was lying in a deck chair
listening to the birds and wondering why the sky was so blue.
It was the kind of afternoon when the whole world seems at
rest. There was hardly a breeze to stir the leaves. There
were no chores to be done and there was plenty of time to
dream. Willie's eyes were just beginning to close drowsily,
when the deck chair wobbled . . . ever so slightly.

"Did I imagine that, or didn't I?" thought Willie. He
didn't have long to wait for an answer. The deck chair
wobbled again.

"I'm getting out of here . . ." said Willie. "Something
funny going on . . ." But because it was hot, he wasn't in a
hurrying mood, and he was still thinking about moving when
he suddenly found himself falling . . . falling . . . falling . . .

"Help," he gulped as he found himself in a dark place,
and face to face with a very surprised looking rabbit.
"Where did YOU come from?" demanded the rabbit.
"From up there . . . I think," said Willie, pointing to
the sky which was now a far away circle of blue.

"What's happened?" Dewy's face had appeared at the edge of the sky. "How did you get down there?"

"He made a hole in the roof of my burrow . . . that's what he did," complained the rabbit.

"Digging a bit close to the surface, aren't you?" asked Basil who had also appeared at the edge of the sky.

The rabbit scratched his head. "I suppose I am now you come to mention it. Should be at least six feet of earth above me. Wait a moment and I'll measure it."

He used one of his long ears as a measuring stick.

"Definitely something wrong here," he said.
"I must have taken a wrong turning somewhere."

"I've got a map indoors," said Basil. "Come inside and we'll have a look at it."

Basil spread the map on the kitchen table and they all studied it carefully.

"I thought I was there . . ." said the rabbit, pointing to a spot on the map which WAS six feet under the surface.

"Well you're not. You're in the middle of our lawn," said Basil. "You took a wrong turning, obviously."

"Most frightfully sorry," said the rabbit.

"You jolly well ought to be," said Willie. "I might have been hurt."

"So might I," said the rabbit. "You could have fallen on top of me."

"Just you make sure you don't make any more silly mistakes," said Willie. "I don't want to fall into a burrow every time I walk across the garden."

Basil rolled up the map and gave it to the rabbit.

"Take this with you," he said. HE didn't want to fall into any burrows either. HE was bigger than Willie. HE might get stuck.

"Thank you," said the rabbit. "That's most frightfully kind of you. I'll get back to my digging now."

"There's just one more thing," said Basil.

"What's that?" asked the rabbit.

"You will fill in the burrow that went wrong, won't you?"

"I'll see to it straight away," said the rabbit. And he did. And by evening it was safe to walk in the garden again.

WILLIE'S SECRET

The birds were only just awake and the early morning sun was only just beginning to glint through the trees when the front door of Ash Lodge opened, very, very quietly, and Willie Mole stepped outside. He trotted quickly down the lane towards the post box.

The postman didn't deliver letters to the door of Ash Lodge. He left them in a box at the end of the lane and Willie was expecting a reply to a letter he had written. "It's come . . . it's come," he whispered excitedly as he lifted a long, narrow parcel from the post box.

He had hoped to sneak back indoors before anyone else was up, but he was too late. Basil was standing at the front door taking in the fresh morning air. Willie gasped and ran round to the back door. He couldn't sneak in that way either. Dewy was in the kitchen getting breakfast. He stood quite still and tried not to panic. What could he say about the parcel? One of them was sure to ask what was in it. Before he could make up his mind what to do Dewy looked up and saw him. Dewy was so surprised to see Willie in the garden, when he had supposed him to be asleep in bed, that he dropped the egg he was supposed to be breaking into the frying pan, onto the floor instead. There was barely time to push the parcel into a hiding place before Dewy flung open the kitchen window and demanded to know what Willie meant by giving him such a fright.

Willie stuck his nose in the air.

"I suppose I can go for an early morning walk if I want to," he said, and marched into the kitchen. "What's for breakfast? I'm hungry. I hope you're not going to give me THAT egg. I like my yolks UNbroken."

"Perhaps he's not feeling very well," said Basil.

"Oh, do stop fussing," said Willie.

"Can't help fussing," said Basil, remembering how difficult it usually was to get Willie out of bed.

"What ARE you doing up so early?" asked Dewy.

"Where have you been?" asked Basil.

"None of your business," said Willie. And no amount of persuading or cajoling would make him tell.

After breakfast, and when he was sure Basil and Dewy were busy elsewhere, Willie rescued his parcel from its hiding place and carried it off into the wood.

Basil worried about Willie all morning. "I suppose he IS alright?" he kept saying.

The tenth time Basil asked the same question, Dewy didn't answer. Instead he asked a question himself.

"Listen," he said. "Can you hear that strange noise?"

There was a shrill . . . hiccupping . . . kind of trill, coming from the direction of the wood.

"Must be some kind of bird," said Basil.

"Let's go and find out," said Dewy, hoping it would take Basil's mind off Willie for a while.

Dewy found the binoculars and Basil wrote a note to Willie to tell him they had gone bird watching, should he come back before they did, and then they crept into the wood.

"We're getting closer," whispered Basil. "What's funny?" he asked, as Dewy began to shake with silent laughter.

"Look there . . ." whispered Dewy, handing the binoculars to Basil. "I spy a . . . Willie-bird."

49

Willie was sitting under a bush blowing on a long wooden pipe. His cheeks were puffing in . . . and out. His chin was wobbling up . . . and down. His whiskers were quivering. His eyes were watering. He was concentrating so hard on what he was doing he didn't hear his two friends creep up behind him.

"BRAVO!" said Basil loudly, right in Willie's ear. Willie stopped in mid-blow. The wooden pipe sailed into the air, and so did Willie. Basil caught the pipe. Willie turned half a somersault and caught his feet in the bush behind him.

"That was clever of you," laughed Dewy.

"You've been spying on me," grumbled Willie, when he had untangled his feet and got over his surprise.

"Couldn't help it," said Dewy. "You can't keep the sort of noise you were making a secret for very long."

"Why didn't you want us to know what you were doing?" asked Basil.

"Because I knew you would laugh at me," said Willie. "And you did . . . didn't you?"

"Only because you were funny," said Basil.

"I would like to have a pipe like that myself," said Dewy, thinking it best to change the subject quickly.

"So would I," said Basil.

"Really?" said Willie, as though he didn't quite believe them.

"Yes! Really!" said both his friends firmly.

So Willie wrote another letter, and got two more pipes. It was much more fun practising together than it had been practising alone. Willie didn't mind how much his friends laughed at him when he could laugh at them. He was glad they had discovered his secret, and so were they.

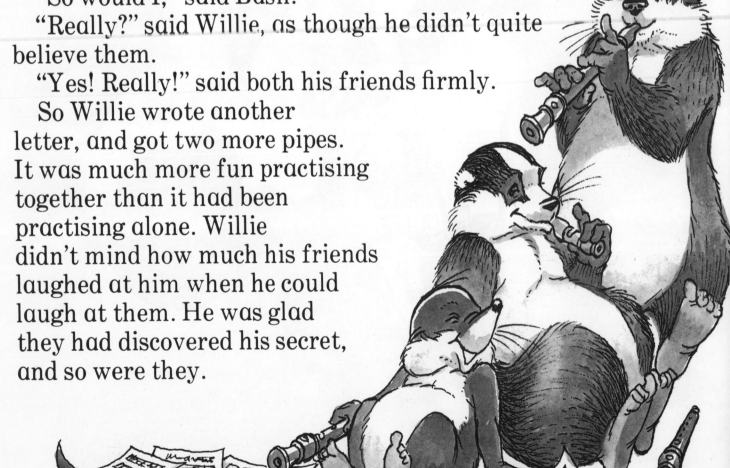

WILLIE DISAPPEARS

Basil was in a thoughtful mood. "I wonder," he said, "what is on the far side of the wood?"

"Whatever it is, it's bound to be something I wouldn't like," said Willie.

"That's silly," said Dewy. "And just to prove it we will go right now and take a look."

Willie protested. He tried to pretend his feet hurt, and then that he had toothache. When that didn't work, he said he had a book he wanted to read, but Basil and Dewy had made up their minds, and so he had to go.

The wood was dark. The trees were tall and leafy, and the undergrowth thick and prickly. Presently they came upon a narrow, winding path. They followed it for a while and then suddenly, as though they were stepping through a doorway, they stepped out of the wood and into the sunshine.

"It's another world," said Willie with a gasp.

"Don't be silly," laughed Basil.

"I tell you it is . . . look, there's a castle . . . I'm going home before someone comes out and casts a spell on me." Willie turned and would have plunged back into the dark wood, but Basil caught hold of his arm.

"Your castle is nothing but an old ruin," he said.
"I don't like it! It's got an eye! It's looking at me!" shivered Willie.
"That's the sun glinting on a window," scoffed Dewy.
"Come on," called Basil. "This looks interesting."

Dewy followed Basil through an ivy covered archway, and because Willie was too scared to stay by himself, he followed too. It was dark and shadowy inside.

"Whoooo aaare yoooo?" wailed a hollow voice that sent shivers darting like arrows down their backs.

"I told you . . . I told you," gasped Willie. Dewy spun round on his heel to tell him to be quiet.

"BASIL!" he cried in alarm. "Willie's gone. IT'S GOT WILLIE!"

Basil shook his fist at the inky shadows. "Put him back! Do you hear? PUT HIM BACK!"

"P p p p p . . ." Dewy's voice had got stuck.

There was a sudden rush of wind and the air seemed to tremble. Dewy had never been so scared in his life. He clung to Basil and pulled him back into a dark corner.

"Did I frighten yooooo?" asked the same hollow voice, this time about an inch away from their heads. "I didn't meeeeen tooooo."

"Wh wh wh what have you done with W W W Willie?" Basil was trying so hard to stop his teeth chattering.

"I haven't done anything with him," said the voice. "Please allow me to introduce myself. I am Albert Owl. I live here. This is my home."

Basil dared to look into a face with enormous, shining eyes, and was glad that he had.

"It's alright Dewy," he whispered, "it really IS an owl. We really are in a ruin."

56

"That's not quite correct," said the owl. "It's a home disguised to look like a ruin. Now, let's see if we can find your friend. He ran off in that direction."

They found Willie crouching against a wall with a curtain of ivy covering everything except his tail.

"I told you it would be something I didn't like," he shivered. "I'm frightened."

"There's no need to be," said Dewy, who had barely got over his own fright. "Let me introduce you to Albert Owl."

"P p p pleased t t t to m m m meet you," said Willie.

"I would be much obliged if you would step inside and take tea with me before you go home," said Albert Owl.

"Thank you," said Basil, "we would like that."

"I wouldn't," said Willie.

"Yes you would," said Dewy firmly. "You will like Albert when you get to know him."

And to Willie's surprise, he did.

THE DUCKLING

One morning, when Basil opened the front door there was a tiny duckling standing on the doorstep.

"Quack," said the duckling forlornly.

"Hallo," said Basil, taking a quick look round outside. "Are you by yourself? Where's your mother?"

Dewy came out to see who Basil was talking to.

"Hallo duckling," he said, "what are YOU doing here?"

"Quack," said the duckling sadly.

"It must be lost," said Dewy. "Stay there young 'un and we'll see if we can find your mother for you."

"Willie!" called Basil. "Come out here and look after our visitor."

Willie came to the door eating a piece of toast.

"Visitor? What visitor? I see no visitor."

"Quack," said the duckling.

"Who said that?" mumbled Willie through a mouthful of toast crumbs.

"He did," said Basil, pointing to the duckling. "Now look after him . . . don't let him go away . . . we'll be back as soon as we can."

"Back? Where are you going?" asked Willie. "You're not going to leave me to look after it by myself . . . are you?"

"He's very little, and he's lost, and we're going to look for his mother. Now you be kind to him."

"You'd better hurry up and find her," called Willie as Basil and Dewy set off in opposite directions. "I might not be very good at this job." He looked the duckling over.

"Funny feathers you've got," he said.

"Quack," said the duckling.

"Is that ALL you can say?" asked Willie. "I suppose you're too young to have learnt much."

"Quack," said the duckling again. "Quack . . . quack . . . " Its little eyes were on Willie's half-eaten piece of toast.

"Oh well," sighed Willie. "I suppose I can always make myself another piece of toast when you have gone. There you are. Don't eat it all at once . . ."

He crumbled the remainder of the toast into crumbs and dropped them in front of the duckling. He stood and watched as it gobbled them up greedily.

"Glad you don't live with us," he said. "Never seen anyone eat a piece of toast that quickly before."

"He will HAVE to live with us for a while," said Basil when he and Dewy came back from their search. "Can't find the little chap's mother anywhere . . . we'll have to look after him."

"You mean, YOU will. I'm not looking after a duckling," said Willie. "I've got better things to do with MY time."

But the duckling had taken
a fancy to Willie, and every
where Willie went, the duckling
went too.

"Shoo . . . shoo . . . go away . . ."
grumbled Willie.

"He's adopted you," said
Basil. "He's chosen you to be
his foster-mother. You should
be very proud."

"Well I'm NOT," said Willie. "I don't WANT to be a duckling's mother." And to prove he meant what he said he hid under his bed. The duckling had no trouble finding HIM.

"I can't understand how it ever got itself lost in the first place," sighed Willie.

Nothing Willie did, or said, upset the duckling in the slightest. Willie had given him some toast so he knew Willie loved him. Every time Willie stood still, he sat on his foot and gazed up at him adoringly. Poor Willie. He didn't KNOW what to do and all Basil and Dewy did was smile.

Late that afternoon there was a knock at the door.

"If that's another duckling, don't let it in," pleaded Willie and he shut himself in the bathroom. The duckling went with him, of course.

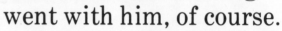

Presently Basil tapped at the door.

"It's alright, you can come out," he called. "It's the duckling's mother. She heard he was here. She has come to take him home."

"And about time too," sighed Willie. "I'm worn out."

"Quack!" said the little duckling when it saw its real mother.

"Qua..qua..qua..quack."
Willie was forgotten.
Willie was relieved.

When the ducks had finally gone and he and the badgers were having supper, Willie said dreamily, "I suppose he was rather sweet . . . I do believe I am going to miss him."

Basil and Dewy did laugh.

WILLIE GOES JOGGING

"Hup, two, three, four . . ."

"Who said that?" asked Willie from inside the woodshed.

"Hup, two, three, four . . ."

"WHO SAID THAT?" demanded Willie, loudly this time.

"There's no need to shout," said a pained voice.
"It's us . . . we're jogging."

Willie looked round the woodshed door. "Oh, it's you
lot," he said, when he saw the ducks running along, one
behind the other, with short bobbing steps. "Why do you DO
that?"

"To keep fit and slim of course," sniffed Ralf Runner
their leader, without getting the tiniest bit out of step.
"You're very podgy . . . you could do with some exercise yourself . . . Hup, two, three, four . . ."

Willie pulled in his tummy and took a deep breath.
"I'll come with you," he said. "I can jog as well as
any duck. I'm extraordinarily fit . . . you'll see . . ."
"Come if you like," said Ralf. "Hup, two, three, four."
"Hup, two, three, four . . ." repeated Willie.

The ducks were used to running. Willie wasn't. It
wasn't long before his breath was coming in short gasps.
  "Can't we slow down a bit?" he puffed.
  "Certainly NOT . . . Hup, two, three, four . . ."
  "Hup . . . puff . . . two . . . puff . . . three . . . puff . . . four . . ."
puffed Willie.

Basil was coming up the lane. He stood to one side to let everyone pass.

"Afternoon," he called to the ducks. "Nice day to go jogging."

"'Tis indeed . . . Hup, two, three, four . . ." replied Ralf, not the slightest bit out of breath.

"And what are YOU doing?" asked Basil as Willie came puffing and waddling along at the rear.

"I'm . . . puff . . . jogging too," said Willie, picking his feet up a bit higher and pulling his tummy in a bit further to prove he WAS extraordinarily fit, and absolutely FULL of puff.

"How far are you going?" called Basil as Willie and the ducks turned from the lane into the road.

"All the way of course," answered Willie's voice faintly, as Willie himself disappeared from view. When the ducks had finished running they marked time together beside the pond.

"Hup, two, three, HALT!" ordered Ralf Runner. They all did, on exactly the same foot, at exactly the same moment. "Dis . . .MISSSSSSSS!"

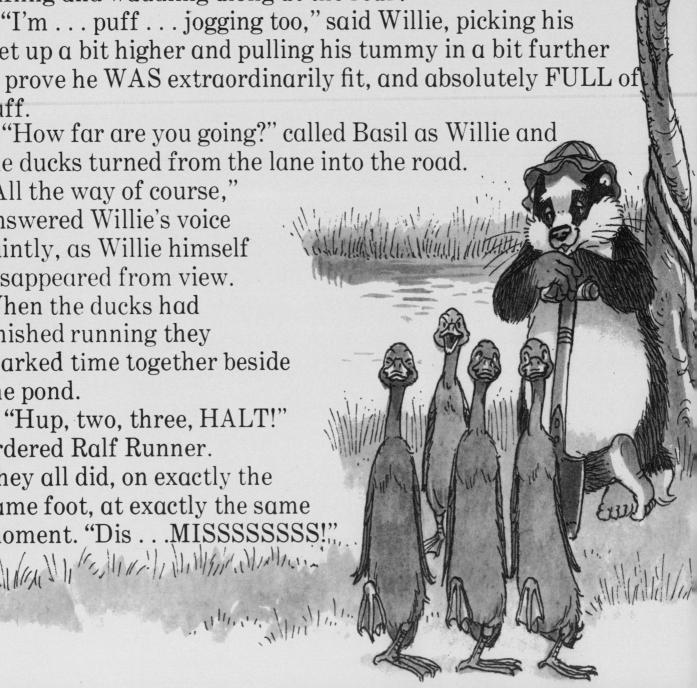

"Where's Willie?" asked Basil as the ducks waddled off in different directions.

"Back there somewhere," said Ralf Runner vaguely, as though it didn't matter where Willie was. Basil put down his spade and called to Dewy.

"Willie's fallen behind . . . I knew he would . . . better get a mustard bath ready for his feet . . ."

Willie arrived home just as it was getting dark. Basil and Dewy were waiting for him in the lane. He was hobbling very, very slowly, as though he was just back from a long, long walk all the way round the world.

"No wonder those ducks call themselves runners," he sighed. "They didn't slow down once . . . just couldn't keep up with them . . . I'm sure my legs are shorter now than when I started."

"Shouldn't have gone in the first place," said Basil.

"Why not?" said Willie indignantly. "I'm as fit as any duck . . . I've got enough puff left inside me to jog another hundred miles."

"You look very tired to me," said Dewy. He put the mustard bath he had prepared, on the floor, in front of Willie's chair. "Put your feet into that," he said. "It will ease the aches and pains."

"It's only my feet that are tired," said Willie as he put his feet into the water and wiggled his toes. "The rest of me is . . . not . . . tired . . . at . . . . . ." He didn't say another word. He couldn't. He had run out of puff. He was fast asleep.

WILLIE BABY-SITS

Willie was walking through the wood one afternoon when he heard voices.

"Let go . . . let go at once," someone was saying crossly.

Willie went to investigate and found Sarah Shrew having trouble with her family.

She had been leading her five little ones, when the one nearest to her, the one holding onto HER tail, had let go and taken hold of a thick stem which was growing up between the leaves instead.

"Why are they doing that?" asked Willie.

"Because they're stubborn and because they're naughty," said Sarah Shrew crossly.

"Because we're tired . . . tired . . . tired . . . tired . . . tired," twittered the little ones. "And can't go a step further . . . further . . . further . . . further . . . further." And they held even tighter to one another, and the one who should have been holding on to Sarah's tail held even tighter to the stem.

"What AM I going to do?" asked Sarah, almost in tears. "How am I going to get them home?"

"Go home," said Willie sternly, to the little shrews, as though that would settle the matter.

"Shan't . . . shan't . . . shan't . . . shan't . . . shan't . . ."

"They're very stubborn," said Sarah. "It's because they are shrews you know."

"I didn't know," said Willie. "Why don't you just leave them there and go home without them?"

Sarah was shocked. "I couldn't possibly do that," she said. "Something might happen to them. They are only babies you know. Someone has to look after them."

"Tell you what," said Willie, who didn't feel like going anywhere himself just then. "You go and get Basil and Dewy, one of them is bound to know what to do, and I'll baby-sit till you get back."

"Are you sure you can manage?" asked Sarah.

"Of course I can. Look at the way they are clinging to that stem. They are not going to go anywhere are they?" What a silly question thought Willie.

"Mind you all behave yourselves," said Sarah as she went.

The little ones said nothing. Willie thought that was because they were tired. He hoped they had fallen asleep, but the instant their mother was out of sight they bounced into life.

"Play . . . play . . . play . . . play . . . play," they squeaked and the one who had been holding onto the stem let go of it so suddenly it twanged backwards and forwards. They swung round in a long line and tried to get behind Willie.

"Catch . . . catch . . . catch . . . catch . . . catch," they cried.

"Don't you dare touch MY tail!" shouted Willie turning to face them. But as fast as HE turned, THEY turned. He couldn't get in front of them and they couldn't get behind him. Round and round they went, round and round, until Willie became so giddy he tripped over his own feet.

"OH!" he cried, his head spinning and his whiskers twitching. "OWWW!!!" he shouted, as sharp little shrew teeth caught hold of his tail. "Let go . . ." he shouted. "Help! HELP!" But no help came and now Willie had a family of shrews attached to HIM.

Very tired shrews they must have been too, for the instant they caught hold of Willie's tail they closed their eyes and fell asleep. Willie was still trying to unfasten them when Sarah Shrew returned with Basil and Dewy. Basil was pushing the wheelbarrow. He looked at Willie and grinned. Dewy wanted to laugh but he didn't dare.

"Help me . . . please . . ." pleaded Willie.

Between them Basil and Dewy lifted Willie and his shrew tail into the wheelbarrow and wheeled him to the shrews' front door. Sarah hurried indoors and began to cook the shrews' favourite food. As the delicious smell of fried mushrooms wafted past their noses they twitched and woke up.

"Mushrooms . . ." they cried, letting go of Willie's tail at once, ". . . mushrooms . . . mushrooms . . . mushrooms . . . mushrooms."

"Bye Willie . . . Willie . . . Willie . . . Willie . . . Willie," they called as they jumped from the wheelbarrow and ran indoors.

"Thank you for bringing my babies home," said Sarah. "I'd invite you all to supper, but you never know . . ." She glanced at Willie and giggled. "They might want to play again . . ."

Willie leapt from the wheelbarrow as though he had been stung by a wasp . . . and ran.

"Goodbye . . ." he called over his shoulder. "I'm not a bit hungry . . ."

"That's the first time I've heard Willie say that," said Basil.

"He'll be hungry again by the time he gets home," laughed Dewy, and Dewy was absolutely right.

LOST AND FOUND

Dewy was re-arranging the store cupboard. Willie was helping.

"Hand me that bag of flour next," said Dewy.

"Look out!" shouted Basil from the other side of the room. "The bo . . ." But he was too late. As Willie handed the bag across to Dewy, the bottom came undone and flour poured onto the rug like a cascading waterfall.

"Atishoo!" sneezed Willie as he was lost in the middle of a white cloud.

"Atishoo!" sneezed Dewy. HE looked like a snowbadger.

"Oh dear," said Basil. "What a mess!"

When the cloud of flour settled there was a layer of white dust everywhere. Basil took charge. Dewy and Willie were sneezing too much to be able to think properly.

"Willie, you take the rug outside and get it clean," he said. "Dewy and I will clean up in here."

Willie pulled the rug out onto the grass and began to whack it with the carpet beater.

Whack! "ATISHOO!" Whack! "ATISHOO!" The harder Willie whacked the bigger the cloud got. It was half an hour before the colours on the rug showed through again.
   "The rug is whacked and so am I," he sighed as he left it on the grass and went indoors to get a drink.

"Willie!" Basil was calling from the garden.
"What is it?" asked Willie, alarmed by Basil's frown.
"You didn't have to beat the rug THAT hard," said Basil accusingly. Willie gasped. There was a large bare patch right in its middle.

"How did that get there?" he asked.

"That's what I want to know," said Basil crossly.

"I didn't do it," said Willie. "It was alright when I left it . . . really it was." And he looked so innocent Basil had to believe him.

"Holes like that don't come by themselves," said Dewy. "I want to know where all the pieces of wool have gone."

"Perhaps the wind blew them away," said Willie.

Dewy tested for wind. "There isn't any," he said.

There wasn't a scrap of coloured wool anywhere on the grass . . . or on any of the bushes . . . or anywhere else.

"Very odd," said Basil, scratching his head. "Very odd indeed. I don't understand this at all."

There was a polite cough behind them.

"Er . . . does this belong to you?" asked a voice. They turned and saw a very embarrassed-looking dormouse. She was struggling with a large bundle of loose woollen pieces.

"They're from OUR rug," said Willie indignantly. "What are YOU doing with them?"

"I think you'd better explain," said Basil sternly.

The dormouse sighed. "It's getting close to the time when we dormice settle down for our winter sleep," she said. "The children were only trying to help. When they saw the rug they thought how snug it would keep us through the winter, so they helped themselves to a little piece of it."

"A little piece . . ." sniffed Willie. "That doesn't look like a little piece to me."

"There's some more of it at home," sighed the dormouse. "I couldn't carry it all. You had better come and get it."

But when they arrived at the dormouse home they found the dormice children already curled up and asleep in a rainbow-coloured bed.

"They didn't waste any time, did they?" said Willie.

They looked so cosy and warm Dewy would not let their mother wake them.

"Let them sleep on," he said.
"But what about your rug?" said the dormouse.
"We'll find something to mend it with," said Basil.
"Don't you worry any more." And that is why one of the rugs
in Ash Lodge has a brown middle and rainbow-coloured borders.

A PROBLEM

The Ash Lodge pond stretches between the trees as though it is part of a winding river. It is possible to walk all round it of course, but more and more often, the badgers and Willie found themselves ferrying their friends across the middle of it, on their raft.

If someone had an errand to do on the far side of the pond, they would call in at Ash Lodge, and drop hints about how much time it would save if only they could go across the pond, instead of round it.

"This is such a useful shortcut," said Hannah Hedgehog as Basil ferried her across one morning.

"I can see that it must be," said Basil, trying not to sigh as Hannah settled herself comfortably. He had been sitting comfortably himself, making plans for the day, when Hannah had called.

"You've no idea how long it used to take me to walk all the way round the edge of the pond," she said brightly. "I've got rather short legs you know. I was always arriving too late for EVERYTHING."

"You won't forget to keep a look out and come across for me when I return, will you?" she said as she stepped ashore.

There were three dormice lazing on the bank.

"Knew you'd come, sooner or later," they said, "didn't feel like walking." They scrambled onto the raft without so much as a by-your-leave and lay on their backs with their tails trailing in the water while Basil did all the work.

"Thanks for the lift, Baz!" they called cheekily as they hopped off on the opposite bank.

"Oh dear," sighed Basil when he got back to the house. "I feel tired already and the day has hardly begun. Perhaps we should sink the raft and put a stop to all this ferrying backwards and forwards."

"We couldn't possibly do that!" exclaimed Dewy. "Our friends rely on us."

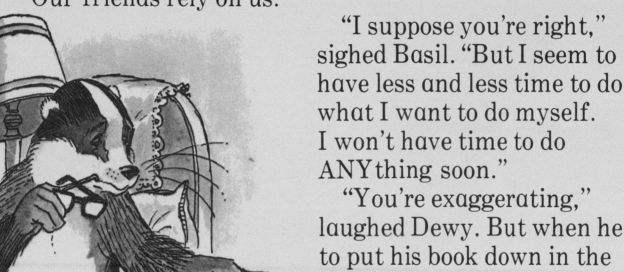

"I suppose you're right," sighed Basil. "But I seem to have less and less time to do what I want to do myself. I won't have time to do ANYthing soon."

"You're exaggerating," laughed Dewy. But when he had to put his book down in the middle of an exciting chapter to go across the pond and bring Hannah back, HE sighed too, and said, "I wish there was another way of crossing the pond."

"Pity there isn't a bridge," said Willie.

"Willie, you're a genius!" cried Basil. "We'll build a bridge."

"Who? US?" asked Willie disbelievingly.

"Do you think we could?" asked Dewy.

"I don't see why not," said Basil.

They asked Otley Otter to help them. He was used to working under water. As they rolled the logs into the pond he roped them together. When there were enough to stretch right across the pond he anchored them firmly, so that they would not float away. They all agreed they could never have made the bridge without his help.

"How would YOU like to be the first to use the new bridge?" Basil asked Otley.

"Well," said Otley, "as you know, I usually swim across the pond, but just this once I think I WILL walk."

"I announce this bridge officially open," he said as everyone followed him across.

Otley promised to keep a special watch on the underneath side of the bridge to see that none of the logs broke loose and he also promised to rescue anyone who was foolish enough to fall off the bridge and into the pond.

"I'll be special bridge-keeper and life guard," he laughed.

For the next few days the bridge was as busy as a town street. Everyone found a good reason for going across at least twice a day and if they hadn't a real reason they made one up. Willie was the one who fell off it, of course. Basil said he would have been MORE surprised if Willie hadn't fallen off. The splash he made as he fell in sent the water bouncing in waves against the banks. It made the logs rock dizzily and frightened all the ducks. Otley managed to catch hold of him before he swallowed too much pondweed.

"How did you manage to do that?" asked Otley as he towed Willie ashore.

"Do what?" spluttered Willie.

"Fall off a perfectly safe bridge."

"I was looking at my reflection," mumbled Willie, "I . . . er . . . sort of . . . er . . . over balanced."

No one ever fell off the bridge again. Not even Willie.
He said once was enough.

And so, once again, the badgers, and Willie, had time
to do the things they wanted to do. When they took the raft
out it was because they felt like a gentle drift in the
dappled shadows and not because someone was in a hurry to
get to the other side of the pond.

The problem had been solved and EVERYONE was happy.

A WET NIGHT

It was a dark night and the lights twinkling from the windows of Ash Lodge were the only stars. The wind was howling. The rain was lashing against the windows and pounding on the roof. One by one the lights went out. Dewy and Basil the two badgers, and Willie the mole, had gone to bed.

Willie tried to shut out the noise of the wind. He put his paws over his ears. That didn't work. He put on his woolly hat. That didn't work either. He was trying to think what to do next when he felt something plop on to his face. Rain was coming in . . . through the ceiling.

"DEWY!" he called loudly, as he tumbled out of bed and switched on the light. "DEWY! BASIL! COME QUICKLY!"

He was standing on his bed trying to catch the drips in a paper cup when Basil appeared in the doorway.

"What is it?" asked Basil with a wide yawn.

"Can't you see! It's dripping!" said Willie crossly. "Do something . . . I can't stand here like this all night."

"I say . . ." said Dewy looking over Basil's shoulder. "There's water coming through the ceiling."

"Help me push Willie's bed against the wall before it gets wet," said Basil. And without waiting for Willie to get down, or even sit down, he and Dewy pushed.

"OOOPS! Sorry!" said Basil. Willie had fallen over backwards and was bouncing up and down as though he was on a trampoline. The drips he had collected so carefully splashed over his face and gave him a sudden cold water wash.

"You might warn me when you're going to do something like that," he spluttered.

"It was an emergency . . . had to act quickly," said Dewy.

"Wind must have blown a slate off the roof," said Basil. "We'll go up and take a look in the morning."

"Why can't you go now?" asked Willie sliding quickly into bed and pulling the blankets round his chin.

"Well, for one thing it's dark," said Basil. "And for another it's raining, and . . ."

"You'll be sorry if you come to wake me in the morning and find I've floated away," said Willie.

"There won't be a flood," laughed Dewy as he put a bucket to catch the drips.

PING . . . PING . . . PING . . . PING . . . PING . . .

"I can't possibly sleep with THAT noise going on," grumbled Willie. But he did.

When he woke it was morning and the sun was shining. It had stopped raining some time during the night, for the bucket was only half full. There was barely enough water in it to make a puddle. Dewy and Basil were outside looking up at the roof.

"I was right," said Basil. "There IS a slate off. We'll get up there and mend it right away."

"What about my breakfast?" asked Willie.

"That will have to wait," said Basil. "Someone must hold the ladder."

Willie got bored holding the ladder and went up onto the roof to see what Basil and Dewy were doing.

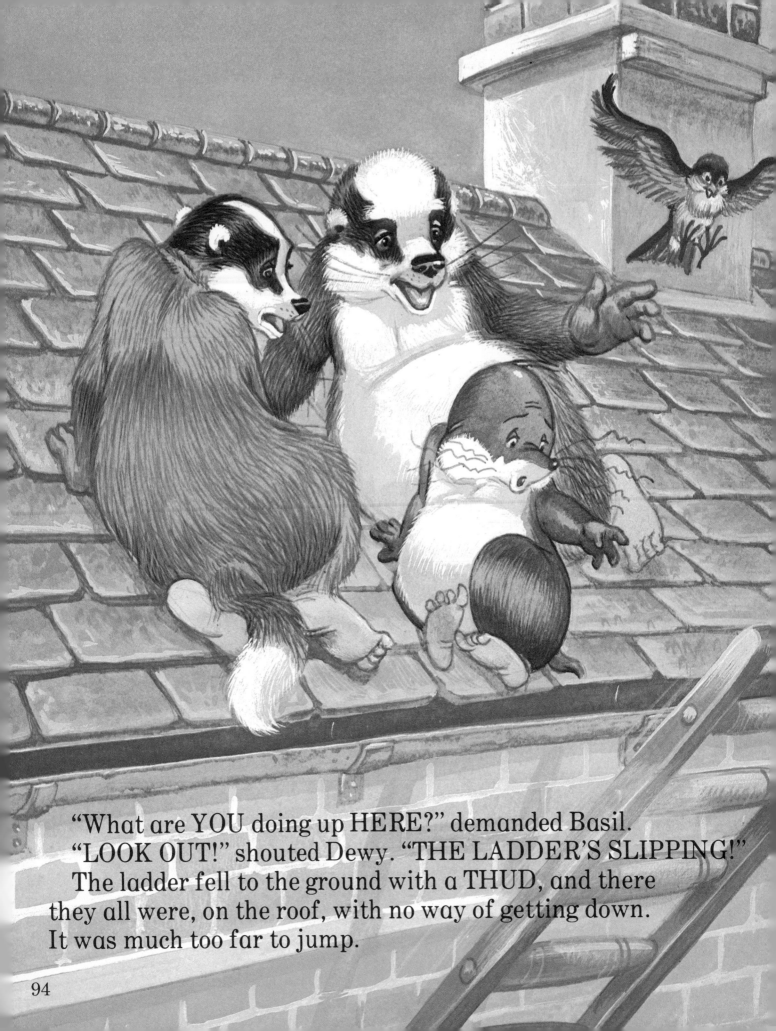

"What are YOU doing up HERE?" demanded Basil.
"LOOK OUT!" shouted Dewy. "THE LADDER'S SLIPPING!"
The ladder fell to the ground with a THUD, and there
they all were, on the roof, with no way of getting down.
It was much too far to jump.

"It's all Willie's fault," said Dewy crossly.
"I don't know why you're fussing," said Willie
brightly. "I'll put it back." And before Dewy or Basil
could stop him he had tucked his legs round the drainpipe
and was sliding towards the ground . . . and the water barrel.

"Oh dear," said Basil quietly as Willie went into the barrel like a cork, and water came out like a fountain.

"Are you alright?" called Dewy anxiously.

"Of course I'm not," spluttered Willie. "I'm WET . . ." He caught hold of the drainpipe and pulled himself out. It wasn't easy. The water ran from his fur in streams and made a pool round his feet. He began to squeeze his fur dry.

"Put the ladder back before you do that," called Basil.

"I might catch cold," said Willie. He made them wait until he had squeezed out the very last drip. THEN he put the ladder back. THEN he remembered he hadn't had breakfast so he stood on the bottom rung and held it steady while Basil and Dewy came down. If he made them TOO cross they might make him get breakfast and that wouldn't suit him at all.

SOMETHING PRICKLY

In the wood the chestnuts were ripening and falling from the trees. Their prickly cases were everywhere.

"Ouch!" said Basil and hopped about on one foot.

"Why don't you look where you're putting your feet," said Willie and then trod on a spiky nutcase himself.

"OUCH!" he said, twice as loudly as Basil.

"Why don't YOU look where YOU are putting YOUR feet," said Basil and Dewy together.

"I suppose you think that's funny," said Willie.

"It is funny," said Basil, carefully avoiding another of the spiky balls.

"What's inside them anyway?" asked Willie.

"Nuts," said Dewy.

"Don't be rude," said Willie. "I asked a perfectly civil question."

"And I gave you a perfectly civil answer," said Dewy. "Nuts . . ."

Willie glowered and puffed out his chest. He looked as though he might explode.

"I'll show you," said Dewy quickly. He picked up a spiky ball that had a split in its coat and prised it open.

He showed Willie the smooth brown nut that had been tucked tightly inside the spiky husk.

"They are very good to eat," he said. He peeled off the brown skin and popped the milky-white nut into his mouth.

"I would like to try one of those," said Willie.

"Then you'd better peel one, hadn't you?" laughed Dewy.
"I suppose you think I can't do it," said Willie and
began to juggle with a ball that seemed to be made from a
million jabbing spikes.
"Ouch! Oh . . . ouch!" he winced.

While Willie juggled and got crosser and crosser but more and more determined not to be beaten, Basil and Dewy gathered a hatful of nuts to take home. At long last, Willie got the nut out of its prickly case. It was very, very tiny and his paws were very, very sore.

"Do you mean to tell me I've gone to ALL that trouble just to get THAT out?" he said crossly. He peeled off the brown skin and put the nut in his mouth. It was gone in one gulp. "They're just not worth the bother," he said.

He was trailing along behind Basil and Dewy, muttering and grumbling to himself when he caught sight of something out of the corner of his eye. He looked quickly at Basil and Dewy. THEY hadn't noticed. He suddenly found something interesting to stop and look at. Then as soon as Basil and Dewy were a safe distance ahead, he scrambled into the leaves and stared with delight at the big, brown prickly ball. It was HUGE. It was GIGANTIC! A prickly something of that size would be worth peeling.

"Ouch . . . oh . . . ouch . . ." he said softly under his breath, as he picked it up and cradled it in his arms. Its prickles were incredibly sharp, but what did that matter? Just think of the size of the nut inside!

He kept his distance behind Dewy and Basil all the way home.

"I'd just like to see their faces when I'm eating this," he said. "But they won't see me because I'll eat it in secret . . ." The prickly ball got heavier and heavier. His tummy began to feel like a pin cushion.

"Where's Willie?" asked Basil when he and Dewy got home.

"He's coming," said Dewy. "I say, he seems to have found something. I wonder what it is?"

"What have you got there?" asked Basil as Willie came round the corner by the shed. Willie was taken completely by surprise. By his reckoning Basil and Dewy should have been safely indoors.

"Where? What? Oh, you mean this," he said, trying to sound casual and unconcerned. He supposed he'd have to share it with them now. "It's a chestnut."

Basil and Dewy stared at him.

"No it isn't," said Dewy.

Willie couldn't argue while he was feeling like a pin cushion, so he put the nut down. And there, right in front of him, it . . . uncurled itself . . . and RAN AWAY.

"Come back!" shouted Willie. "Where do you think you're going?"

"Back to his mother I shouldn't wonder," said Dewy.

"His mother?" Willie didn't understand.

"Don't you know a young hedgehog when you see one?" laughed Basil.

"EEEK!" cried Willie, and all his fur stood on end.
"What WOULD have happened to me if I had tried to peel it?"
He felt quite faint at the thought, but Basil and Dewy
laughed until the tears rolled down their cheeks.
"I don't know why you're laughing," said Willie.
"I don't think it's funny at all."

THE SECRET

Basil had made a bird house and fixed it to a pole in the garden.

"I wish someone would build me a house like that," sighed Willie, as he watched the pigeons move in. He didn't know Basil was standing behind him.

That evening there was a lot of whispering every time Willie left the room. Next morning, as soon as the chores were done, Dewy said, "Get the axe Willie, we're going to do some chopping."

"Do we have to," sighed Willie. He didn't like chopping. It made his back ache. It made him tired.

Basil took him firmly by the shoulder and propelled him outside.

"We need your help," he said. "Now be a good chap and get the axe. We'll be up by the big oak."

Willie knew exactly where the axe was but he spent as much time getting it as he possibly could and then he ambled slower than a snail through the wood.

"You can start there," said Basil, pointing to a thin weedy looking tree. "Chop that down."

"Who? Me?" asked Willie. If he'd known he was going to be the one using the axe he would have taken longer still to find it.

"Yes, you," said Basil. "Dewy and I have got other things to do. When you've chopped that down, you can chop that one . . . and that one . . . and that one . . ." And so that there would be no mistakes, he tied a piece of creeper round each of the four trees. "No slacking, mind . . ."

As soon as Basil and Dewy had gone, Willie put down the axe and sat on a fallen log.

"Cheek . . ." he grumbled. "Leaving me to do the work."

He was still sitting there half an hour later when Dewy and Basil came back with a load of wooden planks.

"Finished already?" asked Basil, though he could see perfectly well Willie hadn't even started.

"Well . . . er . . not exactly . . ." said Willie.

"Well, get on with it then," said Dewy, as he and Basil went off again.

The next time Willie heard them coming back and wasn't caught sitting down. They were carrying the ladder and a piece of rope. They propped the ladder against the trunk of the big oak and Basil climbed up with the rope.

"What are you doing?" asked Willie, leaning on the axe.

"Get on with the chopping," said Dewy.

"I was only asking a simple question . . ." muttered Willie, and he went on mumbling and grumbling to himself all the time he was swinging the axe. "If they're going to be like that I won't bother to ask again," he said to himself.

For some strange reason that Willie couldn't fathom,
Basil and Dewy were hauling pieces of wood into the tree.
"Stop staring and get on with the chopping," called
Dewy. "Those trunks are part of our plan . . . if you keep us
waiting you'll NEVER know what we're doing, will you?"

When all the trunks were cut, Basil tied the rope
round them and hauled them up into the tree too.

"You can bring those smaller pieces up now," he called.

"I seem to be doing twice as much work as anyone else,"
grumbled Willie as he toiled up and down the ladder.

Basil and Dewy made him work in the tree ALL day. Late in the afternoon Basil sent him down to the house to make some sandwiches and a flask of coffee.

"I'm tired," complained Willie. "Can't someone else go?" He couldn't remember the last time he had worked so hard, or for so long, or had such backache. He couldn't understand why Basil and Dewy were looking so cheerful.

"Take your time . . ." called Dewy as Willie plodded off down the footpath.

"Thanks a lot," said Willie. "I suppose that will give YOU time to think of something else for me to do."

He was gone for ages and ages, as Basil and Dewy knew he would be. They were counting on it. They had things to do. As soon as he was out of sight, they set to work like whirlwinds and added all the finishing touches to the day's work.

"Finished . . . just in time," said Basil as they heard Willie coming back.

What a surprise Willie had.

"It's . . . it's . . . a tree house . . ." he gasped. "We've been building a tree house . . . Why didn't you tell me?"

"We wanted it to be a surprise," said Dewy.

"You've been helping us build your own house on a pole," laughed Basil. "We thought as it was going to be your house it was only fair you should do some of the work."

"MY house," gasped Willie. "Is it really MINE?"

"Of course it is," said Basil and Dewy together.

Willie's tiredness, and all his aches and pains, disappeared as though by magic.

"I must be the happiest mole in the world," he sighed, and he looked as though he was too.

A . . . A . . . SOMETHING

Dewy was weeding, Willie was pretending to be busy and Basil was on his knees in the cabbage patch.

"Someone has been eating the cabbages," said Basil.

"It wasn't me," said Willie, quickly swallowing a mouthful of peas and dropping the empty pod.

"Look . . ." said Basil. "Holes in all the leaves.
Now who would do a thing like that?"

"EEEK!" cried Willie as Basil looked up. "You've
got a . . . a . . . something . . . on your nose."

"Have I?" said Basil. "What kind of a something?"

"It's moving . . ." cried Willie. "It's moving . . ."

Basil wrinkled his nose and squinted along towards its tip. "It's only a little caterpillar," he said.

"Only! ONLY a caterpillar! Just let a caterpillar try to crawl on ME!" said Willie. "Just let one TRY, that's all, just let one TRY . . . I'd squash it FLAT!"

"Well don't squash this one, or my nose," said Basil and carefully returned the caterpillar to the cabbage leaf from which it had come.

"I don't think you should do that," said Dewy. "It will repay you by making more holes in the cabbages."

"It's got to eat something," said Basil.

"OOOWWW!" It was Willie again.

"What's the matter now?" asked Basil. "Did a caterpillar touch you?"

"There's one walking on me . . . take it off . . . TAKE IT OFF!"

Basil and Dewy looked. They looked carefully, but they could see nothing remotely resembling a caterpillar . . . unless . . .

"You don't mean THIS, do you?" asked Dewy, picking something green, and fat, from Willie's tummy and dangling it in front of his nose.

Willie closed his eyes tightly.

"I don't want to see it . . . take it away."

"Willie . . ." began Dewy sternly.

"I won't look . . . I WON'T!" said Willie defiantly.

"If you do you will see what . . ."

"I won't . . . I won't . . . I don't want a thing like THAT

getting near MY nose."

"Open your eyes!" ordered Basil.

"Shan't! Won't! Can't! Not going to!"

"If you don't I'll put it back," threatened Dewy.

"You wouldn't dare!" said Willie, but just to make sure he quickly opened one eye and peeped. He closed it again, just as quickly, when he saw Dewy was still dangling the fat . . . green . . . horrible . . . THING . . . in front of his nose.

"We're wasting our time," said Dewy. "I'm going indoors to get supper. I'm taking THIS with me. Willie will have to come indoors too if he wants to see what it is."

"I don't WANT to see it," said Willie and he stood right where he was, with his eyes tightly closed until he was sure Dewy and Basil and the THING had gone.

When it felt safe he opened his eyes and carefully stepped out of the cabbage patch. He was going as far away from cabbage eating caterpillars as he could. How was he to know cabbages weren't the only thing caterpillars lived on. But what Willie didn't see, Willie didn't worry about.

He sat beside the pond until he felt hungry and then he
went to the back door. He knocked loudly.
"YOU don't have to knock," said Basil when he saw who
it was. "YOU live here. YOU can come straight in."
"Not with THAT thing in the house," said Willie.

Dewy appeared beside Basil and held up a jar.

"It's in here," he said.

"Keep it away from me," said Willie, with a shudder.

"It won't hurt you," said Dewy, staring at Willie's head and trying not to giggle. "Here . . . read the label."

Very, very cautiously, Willie leant towards the jar.

"Go on . . . read what it says," urged Basil.

"Dangerous . . ." read Willie with a sharp intake of breath. "Found crawling on Willie. An empty pea pod."

There was a long, long silence as Willie looked at the empty pea pod, and Dewy and Basil looked at the striped caterpillar looping the loop over Willie's head.

"Well, it looked like a giant caterpillar," said Willie at last. "How was I to know it wasn't?"

"All you had to do was open your eyes," said Dewy.

"You should have told me what it was," said Willie.

"We don't have to tell you everything," laughed Dewy, as Basil slipped behind Willie and secretly removed the real caterpillar and put it on a leafy plant. That was something else they wouldn't tell Willie about. He would have made far too much fuss.

TREASURE

Willie had been down the lane to see if there were any letters in the letterbox. He was on his way back when he heard a rustling in the undergrowth. There was something, or someone, throwing leaves and twigs into the air.

"Who's there?" he called, getting ready to run.

"It's me," answered Jake Squirrel from the very centre of a leafy whirlwind.

"What are you doing?" asked Willie.

"What do you think I'm doing? Can't you see I'm looking for something?" Jake Squirrel had more than a hint of crossness in his voice. "Any more silly questions?"

"There's no need to be rude," said Willie. "It's just that you're usually up there," he pointed to the branches above his head, ". . . and so I wondered what you were doing down there."

"Go away and leave me alone," said Jake. "I'm too busy to waste time talking to you."

"Very well," said Willie and continued thoughtfully on his way. 'If Jake Squirrel is looking for something . . .' he thought, 'he must have lost something.' He turned about and went back to where Jake was turning over leaves.

"What have you lost?"
asked Willie politely.
Jake didn't like being
interrupted and shook his fist.
"I've lost my treasure . . .
that's what I've done . . . I've
lost my treasure . . . I dropped
it when I was up there . . . and
now it's down here . . . and
I CAN'T FIND IT!"

"TREASURE!" exclaimed
Willie.
He dived into the leaves
at Jake's feet and began to
throw them into the air. If
there was treasure to be found,
he was joining in the search.
"And what do you think
YOU'RE doing? asked Jake
Squirrel, yanking him to his feet.

"Searching for the treasure of course."

"As long as you remember it's MY treasure when it's found."

"Of course I will," said Willie. "But if it's me who finds it perhaps you'll see your way clear to giving me just a teeny, weeny, little bit of it, for myself."

"I might, and then again, I might not," said Jake. "Now get searching. I'm hungry."

Willie couldn't see what being hungry had to do with finding treasure but he didn't think it wise to ask any more questions at that precise moment.

He'd been throwing leaves around for ten minutes before it occurred to him he didn't know what he was looking for.

"Er, um," he coughed shyly, as though he didn't really want to bother Jake.

"What is it?" asked Jake crossly.

"Er . . . er . . . what does your treasure look like?"

"Brown and round and fat."

"Oh . . ." said Willie. "You didn't mean to say sparkly and shiny and golden, did you?" Sparkly and shiny and golden seemed a much better description of a treasure to him.

"No, I didn't," said Jake. "Now, are you helping me or not?"

"Of course I am," said Willie, though he wasn't quite so sure that he wanted to now. He was almost relieved when Jake threw a bundle of leaves into the air and shouted, "I'VE FOUND IT!"

"Let me see it," cried Willie eagerly. When he saw what Jake was holding he could hardly believe his eyes.

"But THAT'S a NUT!" he said. " A plain, ordinary, common-or-woodland NUT!"

"It might seem plain and ordinary to you," said Jake Squirrel, "but it's treasure to ME. I've been saving it for months. It's the most beautiful nut I have ever found and I am going to eat it on my birthday."

"I would never have stopped to help if I'd known what it was I was searching for," grumbled Willie. "When you said treasure, I thought you meant real treasure."

"Moles are very hard to understand sometimes," said Jake Squirrel.

"So are squirrels!" retorted Willie crossly.

Later that day Willie took out his own treasures, which he kept hidden in a box at the bottom of his wardrobe, and looked at them lovingly, one by one.

"I suppose MY treasures are only treasures to ME," he said. "I wouldn't like to lose any of mine either."

SMOKE

Willie was sitting in his tree house with one eye closed and one eye open. He was looking through his telescope. He could see right over the roof of Ash Lodge and to the wood beyond. There was a wisp of blue smoke curling lazily above the trees.

"See anything interesting?" called Basil from the foot of the tree house ladder.

"Just a wisp of smoke," answered Willie.

"Smoke!" gasped Basil as though seeing smoke was important. He raced up the ladder two steps at a time.

"Show me where." Basil didn't need the telescope. He could see the smoke curling up above the trees without it.

"That needs investigating," said Basil. "Where there is smoke there is bound to be fire."

"Er . . . I'll stay here and keep watch through my telescope . . . er . . . in case it gets worse . . ." said Willie nervously.

"You'll come with me," said Basil firmly. "I may need your help."

"Can't Dewy go with you instead of me?" puffed Willie as he tried to keep up with Basil. Basil could move very fast when he was worried. And he was certainly worried now.

"Dewy's coming too," said Basil. "If the wood is alight we'll need all the help we can get."

Dewy didn't make excuses. He came straight away.

"How do we know where to go?" asked Willie. "We can't see the smoke from down here."

"East," said Basil. Basil had a good sense of direction. If Basil said east then east it was. He led them along the winding paths and turned left and right without a moment's hesitation as though he had a map drawn inside his head.

"He'll get us lost, I know he will," whispered Willie.

Suddenly Basil stopped, and sniffed . . .

"There . . . I knew it . . . I knew it . . ." moaned Willie. "I knew I shouldn't have come . . . we're lost."

"What's that I can smell?" asked Basil, completely ignoring Willie's outburst.

"Smoke," said Dewy.

"Yes . . ." said Basil. "But there's something else . . ."

"Sausages . . ." said Dewy, rather surprisingly.

"It must be a camper." Basil gave a sigh of relief.

"Do you mean there isn't a fire to put out . . ." said Willie, ". . . and the wood isn't going to burn down?"

"I shouldn't think so," said Basil.

"Can we go home then?" asked Willie.

"Not yet," said Basil. "We must make sure."

The smell of cooking sausages got stronger. The crackle of burning twigs became louder. Presently they came to a clearing.

"There's someone sitting there," gasped Willie and tried to turn back the way they had come.

"Sausages don't cook themselves, you know," whispered Basil keeping a firm hold on Willie.

A wily old fox was sitting in front of a campfire cooking sausages in a frying pan.

"I know you're there," he called without turning round. "You might as well come out."

"H . . . how did he know?" whispered Willie as they all stepped into the clearing.

"I heard you whispering," said the fox.

He gave the frying pan a good shake. "Done . . ." he said. "Excuse me while I eat . . . haven't had any breakfast yet."

"Could I . . . ?" began Willie. He couldn't help licking his lips.

"Shush," said Dewy. "Of course you can't . . ."

"Yes he can," said the fox. "You can all have a sausage if you want one, but you'll have to use sticks as forks. I've only got one."

While they all nibbled at the hot sausages which were delicately flavoured by the wood smoke, the fox told them he was a traveller and only passing through that way.

"Never stay anywhere for long," he said. "I like to travel . . . a night here . . . a night there . . . it suits me."

"Where do you sleep?" asked Willie.

The fox pointed to a rolled-up sleeping bag.

"That's all the bed I need," he said. "I sleep under the stars."

"Wouldn't suit me," said Willie.

"Don't suppose it would," said the fox. "But then you're not a fox, are you?"

And though they invited him, the fox wouldn't even stay one night at Ash Lodge.

"The sky is my roof," he said. "That's the way I like it and that's the way I'm going to keep it." And nothing they said would make him change his mind.

RUN WILLIE RUN

Basil had made a walking stick from a piece of gnarled and knobbly wood.

"Do you think I could have it?" asked Willie wistfully. "I've always wanted a walking stick like that."

"Of course you can," said Basil.

Willie was so pleased.

"What are you going to do with it now you've got it?" asked Dewy.

"Go walking with it, of course," said Willie. And he went off into the wood swinging the stick backwards and forwards, trying to keep his feet in step with it as he went. It wasn't as easy as he thought it was going to be. It took a lot of practice to get it right. He found the stick was very good at swishing aside the undergrowth and at holding prickly stems away from his legs. It was also a very good prodder and poker.

"I didn't know a walking stick had so many uses," he said as he pushed it down a hole and twiddled it about. "It's just like having an extra arm." He found another hole to prod and poke.

"Ow!" cried a voice, from somewhere underground.

"Oh dear," said Willie
and tried to pull his stick
from the hole. HE COULDN'T.
Something . . . or someone, was
holding onto the other end.
Suddenly the stick was snatched
from his grasp and something . . .
or someone . . . began to shake it
at HIM.
"EEEK!" cried Willie.

"I'll teach you to poke
sticks down burrows!" shouted
an angry voice, and before
Willie knew what was happening,
he was being chased by an angry
rabbit who was daring to shake
Willie's own stick at Willie
himself.

"Just you wait until I
catch you!" shouted the rabbit.

131

"Help!" shouted Willie. "HELP!"

"Sounds as though Willie's in trouble," said Basil.

"It looks like it too," said Dewy as Willie's roly-poly figure hurtled from the wood with the rabbit in close pursuit.

"I've never seen Willie move so quickly," said Basil. "I wonder what's up."

"Save me! SAVE ME!" shouted Willie.

"Just you wait until I catch you!" shouted the rabbit.

"That rabbit looks angry about something," said Dewy.

It was a very exciting chase to watch.

"I didn't know Willie was so good at dodging out of the way," said Basil.

"I suppose we ought to do something before he gets caught," said Dewy.

"I suppose we should," said Basil and stepped between Willie and the angry rabbit. The rabbit collided with Basil and stopped, very suddenly.

"I don't know why he's chasing me," said Willie hiding behind Basil's broad back. "I haven't done anything."

"Haven't DONE anything!" exploded the rabbit. "Look at that . . . take a look at THAT!" He parted the fur on top of

132

his head and showed them a bump the size of a wren's egg.

"Did Willie do that?" gasped Basil.

"Willie . . ." gasped Dewy. "How could you?"

"I'll tell you how he could," said the rabbit. "He poked this stick down my burrow . . . there I was, sitting in my own armchair, minding my own business, when I was hit on the head with THIS!" He shook the stick angrily.

"You shouldn't do things like that Willie," said Basil reproachfully. "You must apologise at once."

Willie knew he must.

"I'm most terribly sorry . . ." he said. "Really I am."

Basil and Dewy took the rabbit indoors and bathed his bump with cold water. As the swelling went down the rabbit's anger subsided too.

"Ask him if I can have my walking stick back," whispered Willie in Basil's ear.

"I think you should ask him yourself," said Basil.

The rabbit gave Willie back his stick but he made him promise never to poke it down another burrow.

"Don't worry," said Willie. "I wouldn't dare. You might catch me next time."

WAS IT REAL?

Sometimes, when the sun was shining and there were no chores waiting to be done, Willie would take the raft out to the middle of the pond and let it drift while he lay on his back and dozed. One afternoon he woke from a dream and thought for a moment he was still dreaming.

A large grey bird, with legs as long as stilts had flown right over his head. Willie sat up with a jerk and rubbed his eyes. He WASN'T dreaming. It WAS still there. It was paddling in THEIR pond. He had never seen such an important looking bird in the whole of his life.

He didn't dare shout for Basil and Dewy. The bird was sure to hear him. It might be shy and fly away. Even worse, it might be unfriendly and peck him with its long, sharp beak. Very carefully, and so quietly that he made no noise at all, he rowed to the bank. So far so good. He tiptoed towards the house. The heron, for that was what the bird was, took no notice of him at all. It was standing as still as a statue with painted golden eyes.

'Basil and Dewy are never going to believe this,' thought Willie. He could hardly believe it himself.

Basil and Dewy were indoors making lemonade.

"Th . . . the . . . ther . . . there . . ." Willie was so excited he couldn't get the words out.

Basil was squeezing a lemon. The juice kept squirting into his eyes. He was glad of an excuse to stop squeezing for a moment. He looked at Willie with interest.

"What's the matter?" he asked.

"There . . . there's a bird . . . it's got legs as long . . . as long as THAT." By Willie's measurement the heron had legs as long as broom handles.

Basil grinned. "Yes . . ." he said. "I've got that . . . and what else has it got?"

"It's got a neck as long as . . . THAT." By Willie's measurement the heron had a neck as long as a rolling pin.

"I suppose it's got a beak as long as a toasting fork," said Basil.

"Yes . . . yes it has," said Willie.

Dewy had stopped squeezing now. He was staring at

Willie in amazement.

"Do you think he's been lying in the sun too long?" he asked Basil.

"Either that, or his imagination is working overtime," laughed Basil.

"I tell you there IS!" said Willie stamping his foot. "It's simply enormous . . . it's as big . . . as big as YOU."

"Now we know you're exaggerating," laughed Dewy.

"I'm NOT!" said Willie.

"You are . . ." said Basil. "Stop making up stories and come and squeeze some lemons . . . you'll probably drink most of the lemonade when it's made anyway."

"Shan't!" said Willie, and he stormed out of the house looking like a thunder cloud.

He marched angrily to the
pond and faced the heron. He
didn't care if it did peck him.
"They don't believe you
are real," he said. "They
think I'm making you up."
And just to prove to himself
that he wasn't, he dared to
touch the heron's spindly leg

The heron turned and gave him a long, haughty stare.

"You ARE real . . . aren't you?" said Willie.

"Of course I am," said the heron. "But are YOU real, you funny creature, that's what I would like to know?"

And without waiting for an answer the heron spread its wings and flew away.

Willie stood and stared
until the heron was just a
tiny speck in the sky.

"Well . . ." said a voice
at his elbow. "Where is it?"

Willie nearly jumped out
of his skin. Basil and Dewy
had crept up behind him and
were grinning from ear to ear.

"Where's what?"

"This bird that's got legs
like broom handles . . ."

"It's gone," said Willie.

"We thought perhaps it
might have done," said Basil
with a sly wink at Dewy.

"I told you he was
dreaming," said Dewy.

"I wasn't," said Willie.
"I spoke to it. It told me
itself it was real."

"Some of us will believe
anything," laughed Basil.

"And some of us believe
nothing at all," sighed Willie.

A NIGHT OUT

Something had jumped across the path and under a leaf, right in front of Basil and Willie. Something tiny.

"It's a jumping stone!" shrieked Willie.

"Don't be silly, stones don't jump," said Basil. He lifted the leaf to see what it was that was trying to hide.

"OWWW . . .!" shrieked Willie as the tiny thing jumped again.

"Stop doing that . . . you'll frighten it," said Basil.

"It's frightening ME," said Willie. "But I suppose that doesn't matter."

"It's a baby frog," said Basil. "Look!" He had picked up the tiny thing. "Take a peep, it won't hurt you."

Willie dared to look . . . and the tiny frog jumped again.

"OW!" shrieked Willie, jumping half a yard into the air. "It punched me on the nose."

"Sometimes . . ." sighed Basil, ". . . you are SO silly."

"Spiteful thing," said Willie. "Jumping about like that and throwing punches when a mole least expects it . . . it shouldn't be allowed."

"Look! There's another," said Dewy. "And another." There were little frogs everywhere.

Everywhere Willie stepped a frog jumped out at him.
And every time a frog jumped, Willie jumped as well.
"Where have they all come from?" he wailed.
"From the pond of course," laughed Basil. "The
tadpoles have grown their legs."

"There are millions of tadpoles in the pond," gasped
Willie. "Do you mean to tell me they're ALL going to turn
into frogs?"

"Probably," said Basil. Without saying a word Willie
dived through the shed door and banged it shut behind him.

143

"What are you doing in there?" called Basil through the window.

"I'm staying here till all those frogs have hopped away," said Willie.

"I do believe he's afraid of them," said Dewy.

"I'm NOT!" said Willie. But he was still in the shed at bedtime.

"Have they all gone?" he called through a crack in the door.

"How can we tell?" said Basil. "It's dark out here."

"They're probably asleep," said Dewy. "Be brave Willie, make a run for it . . ."

"I might," said Willie. "Then again I might not . . . they might all be waiting out there to pounce on me . . . no . . . I've decided . . . you can bring my bed out here . . . I'll be much safer here . . ."

"You'll have to make do with the camp bed," said Basil. "If you want to sleep in your proper bed you can jolly well come indoors."

"I don't know why YOU'RE grumbling," grumbled Willie. "I'm the one who is under attack." He opened the shed

door just wide enough for them to push the camp bed through the gap, then shut it again quickly. He didn't sleep very well. In fact he hardly slept a wink. The walls of the shed kept creaking. Once he thought he heard something squeak. He could hear someone breathing but he thought that was himself.

"Perhaps I should have gone indoors," he sighed, as the first light of morning shone through a knot hole.

"Why? Don't you like it here?" asked a deep, gravelly voice, from somewhere under the camp bed. "I ALWAYS sleep here . . . I find it very comfortable."

Willie's shriek almost blew the roof off the shed. He almost pushed the door off its hinges in his hurry to get out. He ran across the garden and banged at the back door shouting, "Let me in . . . LET ME IN . . ."

It took a hot drink and a piece of Dewy's chocolate cake to calm him down.

"There . . . there's someone in the shed . . ." he said. "They . . . they've been there ALL night . . . with MEEEE!"

Basil and Dewy went at once to investigate. When they saw who the intruder was they invited him to the house.

"Meet Grandpa Frog," said Basil with an enormous grin.
"Pleased to meet you, again," said the frog.
Willie recognised the voice and fainted clean away. He
had run away from the tiny baby frogs and spent the whole
night with an ENORMOUS GIANT of a frog under his bed!

BEGINNERS PLEASE

The weather was getting colder. Much colder. One morning, there was a thick white frost covering everything in icy lace.

"Come out here and take a look," called Basil.

"Ow!" cried Willie as he slipped on an icy patch.

Basil helped him to his feet.

"I should try to go round the icy patches if I were you," he said.

The ducks came waddling across from the pond. They looked very unhappy.

"Isn't it slippery?" said Willie cheerfully.

"You don't have to tell US that," they quacked crossly. "We know already . . . we've all got bruises to prove it."

"Oh . . ." said Willie. "Did you slip too?"

"Slip . . . slip . . ." they quacked. "We've done nothing else but slip." One of them held out a webbed foot. "See that . . . that's for swimming with . . . not for sliding on . . ."

"Then why don't you swim with it?" Willie was puzzled.

"Can't swim without water."

Willie laughed. "You've got a pond full of water."

"That's what you think," quacked the ducks. "Just take a look at the pond."

So they did. It was covered from bank to bank with a thick layer of ice. There wasn't enough water for a duck to get a foot in, let alone sit down and swim.

"What's to be done?" asked the ducks.

"I'll show you what's to be done," said Basil. He went to the shed and came back with a wooden mallet.

CRASH went the mallet onto the edge of the ice. The ice cracked. CRASH went the mallet again. The ice splintered and broke. Basil chipped away at the broken edge until there was a hole big enough for the ducks to swim in.

"Quack . . ." they said. "Thanks very much Basil. Oh what a relief it is to get our feet back into the water." And they paddled round and round quacking happily, not caring a jot how cold the water was.

Basil picked up a piece of the broken ice.

"It's very thick," he said.

"Thick enough for US to slide on?" asked Dewy hopefully.

"I'm sure it is," said Basil and stepped onto the pond.
"Basil . . . DON'T!" Willie covered his eyes and waited
for the splash. It didn't come.
Swish . . . sh . . . sh . . . went Basil across the ice.
Swish . . . sh . . . sh . . . went Dewy after him.

"You'll never get ME on there," said Willie. But
Basil and Dewy seemed to be having such a good time he said
he would give it a try if they promised to help him.

"Hold me," he said. "Don't let me fall." They held
him SO tightly he couldn't have fallen if he had wanted to.

"Try it on your own now," said Basil, when Willie had had a few practice slides.

"Wheeee!" cried Willie. "OOOOH!" cried Willie as he wobbled. "OWWWW!" cried Willie as he fell.

"You're supposed to stay on your feet," laughed Dewy as Willie slid across the pond on his tail.

"I know I am . . ." grumbled Willie. "I suppose you think I did that on purpose."

Basil and Dewy helped him to his feet.

"Try again . . ." they said.

"I don't want to," said Willie. But they gave him a gentle push and this time he managed to stay on his feet.

"I can do it . . . I can do it . . ." he cried. Now he knew he COULD slide, he practised and practised, and though he fell over dozens of times he really began to get rather good.

"You're cleverer than you think," said Dewy.

"You mean I'm cleverer than YOU think," said Willie.

It stayed very cold all day. News that the pond was frozen spread very quickly and everyone was invited to join in the fun.

"Beginners this way please . . ." said Willie. "I'll show you what to do. Now just watch this . . . it's very easy." And to prove that it was, he gave a demonstration glide. It was straight and very fast. He swished to a very neat halt and was immediately surrounded by his eager friends.

"Please show US how to slide like THAT!" they said.

"You should have seen him this morning," laughed Basil.

"I'm sure I don't know what Basil's talking about," said Willie. "Now, let's get started. Come with me."

There was fun and laughter all the afternoon and when it was too dark to slide without bumping into one another, everyone crowded indoors. Basil roasted chestnuts, Dewy made hot soup and Willie cut thick slices of bread to dip in the soup when it was ready. Everyone was VERY happy.

THE RESCUE

Willie was sitting on a branch which reached out over the pond, and dreaming about summer, when he heard a cry for help. He leant over and looked into the water. Before he knew what was happening, two little paws had reached up and caught hold of his.

"Oooeerrr!" cried Willie, and would have fallen into the water himself, but was saved because two more paws reached up from BEHIND and caught hold of his feet.

"Help!" cried Willy. "HELP!"

Basil and Dewy heard his cries and came running.

"What ARE you doing?" they asked when they saw him looped over the branch with a rabbit hanging from each end.

"He's rescuing US!" chorused the two rabbits. "We got too close to the edge and fell in. Willie's a hero!"

"He needs rescuing himself now," laughed Basil.

"I'll get the fishing net," said Dewy, and couldn't resist adding before he went, "Hang on. Don't go away."

"We'll take the one in front first," said Dewy when he returned. "Make sure you hang on," he said to Willie.

"I can't think why you keep making silly remarks like that," said Willie.

"Let go, NOW!" called Dewy, and the rabbit who was holding onto Willie's paws let go and dropped into the net.

"Oooeerrr!" cried Willie as he found himself being pulled backwards by the weight of the second rabbit.

"Hang on!" shouted Basil and Dewy urgently.

"I am! I am!" cried Willie. And he was . . . like a limpet. "You might have warned me that was going to happen," he said, when he had got over the surprise.

"I did," said Dewy.

The second rabbit dropped into the net and was lifted to safety. That left Willie.

"What about me?" he called.

"You don't need us. You can get down by yourself," said Basil. "Crawl backwards along the branch."

"I'm not doing THAT!" declared Willie. "You'll have to catch ME in the net."

So, Willie dropped into the net too. Head first.

SPLASH!!! Willie was heavy, and though Basil and Dewy really did try they could not hold the net steady. It dipped down into the water.

"I knew that would happen," sighed Basil.

"You did that on purpose," spluttered Willie as the rabbits helped lift the net to the bank.

"Heroes aren't supposed to grumble," said Basil.

"Am I really a hero?" asked Willie.

"Of course you are," said Dewy. "Even if you did have to be rescued yourself."